MW01132671

Israel

Denise Allard

RSVP

RAINTREE
STECK-VAUGHN
P U B L I S H E R S
The Steck-Vaughn Company

Austin, Texas

Published by Raintree Steck-Vaughn Publishers, an imprint of Steck-Vaughn Company

A ZOË BOOK

Editors: Kath Davies, Pam Wells
Design: Sterling Associates
Map: Julian Baker
Production: Grahame Griffiths

Library of Congress Cataloging-in-Publication Data

Allard, Denise, 1952-
    Israel / Denise Allard.
        p. cm. — (Postcards from)
    "A Zoë Book" — T.p. verso.
    Includes index.
    Summary: A collection of fictional postcards, written as if by young people visiting Israel, describes various sights and life in the modern Jewish state of Israel.
    ISBN 0-8172-4020-9 (hardcover). — ISBN 0-8172-6203-2 (softcover)
    1. Israel—Description and travel—Juvenile literature.
    [1. Israel—Description and travel. 2. Postcards.] I. Title. II. Series.
DS107.5. A44 1997
956.94—dc20   96–2610
                                                                          CIP
                                                                           AC

Printed and bound in the United States
1 2 3 4 5 6 7 8 9 0 WZ 99 98 97 96

Photographic acknowledgments

The publishers wish to acknowledge, with thanks, the following photographic sources:

Eitan Simanor - cover r, 24, / Andrea Stern - cover bl; / Fred Friberg 10; / Israel Talby 16; / Adina Tovy 20; / Robert Harding Picture Library; The Hutchison Library / Nancy Durrell McKenna – title page, 14; / Sarah Errington 18; Impact Photos / Caroline Penn - cover tl; / Christophe Bluntzer 6; / John Cole 8; / Mark Cator 12, 26; / Alan Keohane 22; Zefa 28.

The publishers have made every effort to trace the copyright holders, but if they have inadvertently overlooked any, they will be pleased to make the necessary arrangement at the first opportunity.

Contents

All the words that appear in **bold** are
explained in the Glossary on page 30.

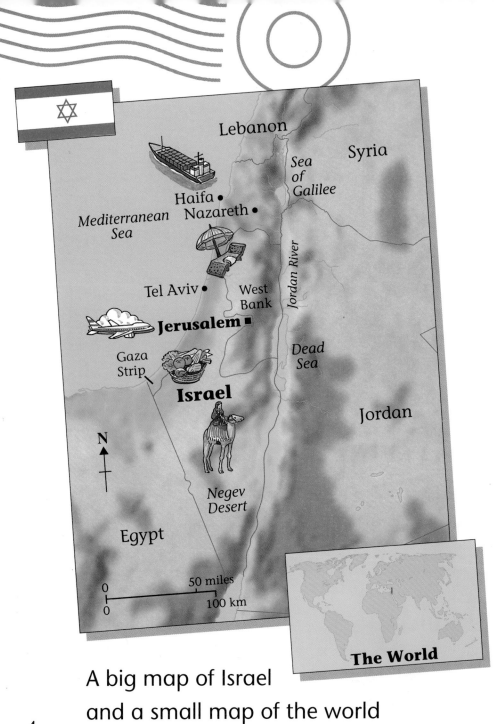

Lebanon

Syria

Sea
of
Galilee

Haifa •
Nazareth •

Mediterranean
Sea

Jordan River

Tel Aviv •
West
Bank

Jerusalem ■

Gaza
Strip

Dead
Sea

Israel

Jordan

N

Negev
Desert

Egypt

0   50 miles
├────────────────┤
0   100 km

The World

A big map of Israel
and a small map of the world

4

Dear Alex,

Israel is not a big country. You can see it marked in red on the small map. The plane took 12 hours to fly here from Chicago. It is hot and sunny in Israel.

Love,

Naomi

P.S. Mom says that Israel became a country in 1948. My grandparents moved to Israel with many other Jewish people. My dad was born here. He can speak the Jewish language called Hebrew.

The Dome of the Rock, Jerusalem

Dear Laura,

Jerusalem is a **holy** city for many people. There are special places in the Old City where people go to pray. People who follow the religion of **Islam** pray at the Dome of the Rock.

Love from,

Ali

P.S. Mom says that most Arab people in Israel follow Islam. They speak in Arabic. Most people speak English and Hebrew or Arabic. Each language uses a different kind of writing.

A hot food stand in Jerusalem

Dear Natasha,

Today we went to the market. People were selling hot snacks from street stands. I bought some peaches. Dad gave me some Israeli money called *shekels* to pay for them.

Your friend,

Anna

P.S. We are going to a Jewish **restaurant** today. Dad says that Jewish food is prepared in a special way that makes it *kosher*. *Kosher* is a Hebrew word that means pure.

Floating on the Dead Sea

Dear Joseph,

We are staying beside the Dead Sea. It is very hot here. The water is so salty that you cannot sink. It is really fun! Some people think that the water will make them feel better.

Your friend,

Bob

P.S. Dad says the Dead Sea is so salty that nothing can live in it. There are no fish and no plants in the water. That is why it is called the Dead Sea.

Some children catch the bus to go to school

Dear Amy,

Cities are close together in Israel. The roads are good, so many people travel by car. We travel by bus from city to city. There are lots of buses. They are always full of people.

Your friend,

David

P.S. Mom says that the Jewish people in Israel follow a religion called **Judaism**. Saturday is a holy day for Jewish people. They stay at home. The buses do not run.

Children working on a *kibbutz*

Dear Ruth,

We are staying with my cousin Daniel. He lives on a *kibbutz*. A *kibbutz* is a village where many families live together. They farm the land together, too. Everyone works, even the children.

Your friend,

Emma

P.S. Daniel says after school he helps feed the animals. Babies go to a nursery while their mothers work on the farm.

Games on the beach near Tel Aviv

Dear Robin,

The city of Tel Aviv is on the coast. It is full of modern hotels and big office buildings. We spent today on the beach. It was very crowded. Tomorrow we are going shopping.

Love,

Lucy

P.S. We are going to visit the old city of Jaffa. Mom says that Tel Aviv and Jaffa are very close together. In fact, Jaffa is really part of Tel Aviv.

Inside a church in Nazareth

Dear Martin,

We are in Nazareth. This is a special town for people who follow the **Christian** religion. They come from all over the world to visit the churches here.

Love,

James

P.S. Nazareth is in the northern part of Israel. Many Arab people live here. Aunt Ruth says that most people who visit Nazareth go to a Christian church to pray.

A view of Haifa, from Mount Carmel

Dear Rachel,

We have reached the town of Haifa. It is on the side of a steep hill called Mount Carmel. An underground train took us to the top of the hill. We saw the **harbor** down below us.

Love,

Vicky

P.S. There were lots of big ships in the harbor. Mom says that the ships take fruit and vegetables all over the world.

Camels in the Negev Desert

Dear Bruce,

We are not far from the border of a country called Egypt. This is the Negev **Desert**. It hardly ever rains here. The farmers use river water to help their **crops** grow.

Love,

Sandra

P.S. Dad says parts of the desert are very dry. No crops will grow there. The Bedouin people live here. They go from place to place in the desert with their animals.

Canoeing on the Sea of Galilee

Dear Simon,

The people of Israel are good at many sports. They like to spend time outdoors. They enjoy swimming, windsurfing, and canoeing. They also play tennis, football, and golf.

Love,

Josie

P.S. Mom says that people go camping and walking in special parks. The birds and the wild animals that live in these parks are **protected**.

Saying prayers at the Wailing Wall in the Old City, Jerusalem

Dear Gary,

This Jewish boy is praying at the Wailing Wall. The wall stands where a **temple** used to be. People write prayers on a piece of paper. They push the paper into the wall.

Your friend,

Steve

P.S. Dad says that there are many **festivals** in Israel. Some are part of the Jewish and the Christian religions. Others are part of the religion of Islam.

The flag of Israel

Dear Sima,

The blue star on the flag stands for the Jewish religion. It is called the Star of David. King David lived in Israel over 2,500 years ago. He was the first king of the Jews.

Love,

Alan

P.S. Dad says that Israel is ruled from the **capital** city, Jerusalem. The people choose their own leaders, so Israel is a **democracy**.

Glossary

Capital: The town or city where people who rule the country meet. It is not always the biggest city in the country.

Christians: People who follow the teachings of Jesus. Jesus lived about 2,000 years ago.

Crops: Plants that farmers grow. Most crops are grown to make food.

Democracy: A country where all the people choose the leaders they want to run the country

Desert: A very dry place where it hardly ever rains

Festival: A time when people remember something special that happened in the past

Harbor: A place where ships can dock for safety

Holy: Something to do with religion

Islam: People who follow the religion of Islam are called Muslims. They live by the teachings of Muhammad. Muhammad wrote down the laws of God for Muslims about 1,400 years ago.

Judaism: The religion of people who follow the teachings of Moses. Moses wrote down the laws of God for Jewish people about 4,000 years ago.

Protected: Kept safe. People are not allowed to pick wild plants or to hunt wild animals in special parks. The wildlife is protected, so it does not die out.

P.S.: This stands for Post Script. A postscript is the part of a card or letter that is added at the end, after the person has signed it.

Restaurant: A place where people go to eat meals. People pay for the food they eat there.

Temple: A building where people go to pray

Index